# Paper Mice

Written by
## Megan Wagner Lloyd

Illustrated by
## Phoebe Wahl

*A Paula Wiseman Book*
SIMON & SCHUSTER BOOKS FOR YOUNG READERS
NEW YORK  LONDON  TORONTO  SYDNEY  NEW DELHI

With a snip and a clip,
and a clip and a snip,
the paper mice were made.

DELLA

With the dot and the swirl of a slender brush,
sharp, bright eyes appeared, tiny noses,
elegant whiskers, and perfect names.
And then they were placed between the pages
of two books, pressed flat, and put away.

They were only paper mice, but even they knew
that night is a mouse's day,
and a time to roam free of fright.
"Come!" the house seemed to call. "There is
much to explore!"

Neither one noticed the other. They were both so very busy breathing in the brand-new smell of the house and drinking in the brand-new sight of the night.

Away dashed Della.

Off tiptoed Ralph.

Della paused.
She felt so small,
and everything else was so big.

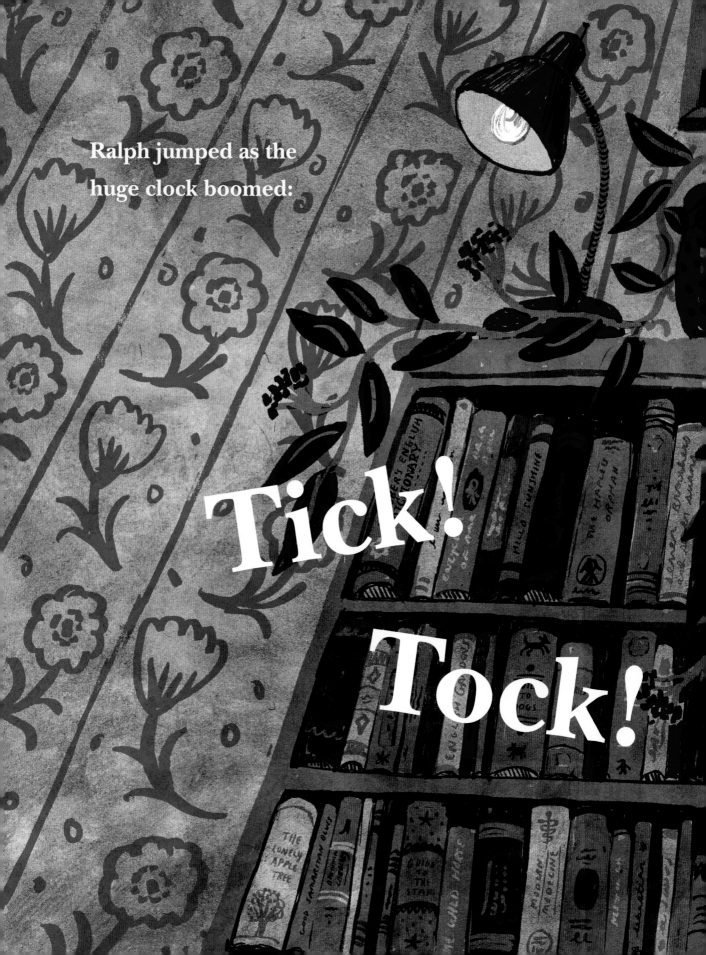

Ralph jumped as the
huge clock boomed:

Tick!

Tock!

**Up and down . . . and all around . . .**

the paper mice adventured.

**Ralph crept along, curiosity tugging him forward.**

Della scampered on, wondering what she'd find around the next corner.

*Why, this house is just my size!* she thought.

*If only I had an extra pair of paws,*
thought Ralph.
He pulllllled and pulllllled—

**and slipped!**

What was that?
Della was sure
she saw something move.

With the pop and the glow of the last of a fire,
Ralph dried himself to the tip of his tail. . . .

And with a shout and a shove
Della pushed him out of the way of a sizzling spark!

"Oh!" gasped Ralph. "Th-thank you!"

"You're welcome!" Della beamed. "I'm Della."

"M-my name's Ralph," Ralph stammered.

The paper mice both smiled . . .
and off they went!

Here and there . . .

this way and that way . . . Della and Ralph ran.

A second set of paws, it turned out,
made everything easier . . .
not to mention more fun!

The house creaked,
the fire sighed,
the night slipped away,
and the mice were happy.

Out into the darkness they'd each ventured—alone—
and found true comfort: a friend.

And as the clock sang the hour,
paper paw met paper paw,
and before the night gave way to day,
Della and Ralph danced.

And then,
with the yawns of two tired mice,
they slipped back between
the pages of their books,

**and fell asleep.**

*For Nelle*
—M. W. L.

*For Jenn, with thanks for the*
*encouragement and support*
—P. W.

SIMON & SCHUSTER BOOKS FOR YOUNG READERS
An imprint of Simon & Schuster Children's Publishing Division
1230 Avenue of the Americas, New York, New York 10020
Text copyright © 2019 by Megan Wagner Lloyd • Illustrations copyright © 2019 by Phoebe Wahl
All rights reserved, including the right of reproduction in whole or in part in any form.
SIMON & SCHUSTER BOOKS FOR YOUNG READERS is a trademark of Simon & Schuster, Inc.
For information about special discounts for bulk purchases, please contact
Simon & Schuster Special Sales at 1-866-506-1949 or business@simonandschuster.com.
The Simon & Schuster Speakers Bureau can bring authors to your live event. For more information or to book an event,
contact the Simon & Schuster Speakers Bureau at 1-866-248-3049 or visit our website at www.simonspeakers.com.
Book design by Chloë Foglia • The text for this book was set in New Baskerville.
The illustrations for this book were rendered in cut paper, watercolor, and digitally.
Manufactured in China • 0319 SCP
First Edition
2 4 6 8 10 9 7 5 3 1
Library of Congress Cataloging-in-Publication Data
Names: Lloyd, Megan Wagner, author. | Wahl, Phoebe, illustrator.
Title: Paper mice / Megan Wagner Lloyd ; illustrated by Phoebe Wahl.
Description: First edition. | New York : Simon & Schuster Books for Young Readers, [2019] | "A Paula Wiseman book."|
Summary: One night, two newly made paper mice separately explore a dark house,
finding each other along the way and discovering a shared love of adventure.
Identifiers: LCCN 2017015127| ISBN 9781481481663 (hardcover) | ISBN 9781481481670 (eBook)
Subjects: | CYAC: Mice—Fiction. | Friendship—Fiction.
Classification: LCC PZ7.1.L59 Pap 2018 | DDC [E]—dc23
LC record available at https://lccn.loc.gov/2017015127